ROODICA THE RUDE

Who stole the River?

CATNIP BOOKS
Published by Catnip Publishing Ltd.
14 Greville Street
London EC1N 8SB

First published 2010
1 3 5 7 9 10 8 6 4 2

A CIP catalogue record for this book is available from the British Library.

ISBN 978-1-846470-74-5

Printed in Poland

www.catnippublishing.co.uk

ROODICA THE RUDE

Who stole the River?

MARGARET RYAN

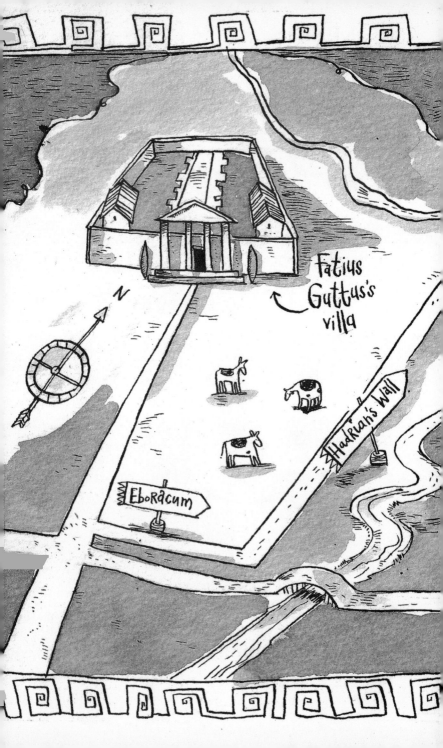

To Ewan, with love

Long, long, ago...

Back through the swirling mists of time when wolves and bears and wild boar roamed the land, and underpants hadn't been invented, the Romans thought it would be a 'superba idea' to invade Britain. The people of Britain, or Celts as they were then called, thought this was a rotten idea and fought back.

Thump! Thud! Wallop! Ouch!

But despite that, the Romans won.

(Romans 1 - Celts 0)

And the Romans stayed. They built fine houses, straight roads and taught washing. "Don't forget to wash behind your ears, o stinkius peasant!"

They also collected taxes. Lots of taxes. King Bren of Brensland didn't like the taxes or the Romans. He preferred going off to war. So he did. Trouble was, he left his wife, Queen Goodica, and their three daughters, Foodica, Woodica and Roodica behind to fend for themselves…

Roodica's Royals (The Celts)

KING BREN

King of Brensland

Likes fighting, fighting and fighting. Oh, and wars, where he's usually to be found, right in the middle of the fighting.

QUEEN GOODICA

Queen of Brensland

Likes peace and quiet.

Lives at Maiden Castle trying to bring up her three daughters as proper princesses.

PRINCESS FOODICA

Princess Foodica

The eldest daughter and a proper princess. She's always neat and tidy, never says anything wrong, and is a wonderful cook.

9

Princess Woodica

The middle daughter and
a proper princess. She's always
sweet and gentle, never does
anything wrong, and makes wonderful
things out of wood.

Princess Roodica

The youngest daughter and a proper…pain in
the posterior. She's never neat and tidy, never
sweet and gentle, and is
always saying and doing
everything wrong. Her
mother wonders what on
earth she'll do with her.

Roodica's Friends

Fleabag, the wolfhound

He goes everywhere
with Roodica.

Plodette, the pony

She carries Roodica
around sometimes.
Slowly.

Gideon, the horse boy

He tries to keep Roodica
out of trouble.
Fat chance!

The Terrible Togas (The Romans)

Magnus Maximus (Big Max)

Very superstitious Roman
Governor. Likes ordering
people about and getting
presents. Wishes someone would
hurry up and invent underpants
as he finds Britain rather chilly.

Fatius Guttus (Fat Gut)

Tax Collector (Boo Hisssss).
Likes collecting taxes, taxes,
and more taxes, especially
from those crummy Celts.
Also likes eating, drinking
and burping loudly.

Copius Mucus (Lottasnot)

Son of Fatius Guttus.
Likes telling tales,
sneaking up
on people
and sniffing.

Lesson day. Oh no!

It was lesson day at Maiden Castle and Princess Roodica was not happy. She turned over on her little rush bed, pulled up the bearskin cover and closed her eyes tight shut.

"I'll waken up tomorrow when lesson day is over," she decided.

No chance. Fleabag jumped on her and licked her nose. **SLURP!**

"Get off, Fleabag!" Roodica yelled. "Your breath smells like a badger's bum."

"Princesses shouldn't be so rude," said her oldest sister, Foodica.

"Princesses should be polite," said her older sister, Woodica.

"Polite's boring," yawned Roodica. "And so's lesson day. I'm going back to sleep."

And she closed her eyes and did some pretend snoring.

SNORK
SNORK
WHISTLE
WHISTLE
WHEE

But it didn't work.

Her mother, Queen Goodica, climbed up the ladder from the big hall into the princesses' bedroom.

"Stop that silly noise immediately and get dressed, Roodica," she said. "Gideon's been here since dawn and now Druid Big Brain has arrived. He's keen to start today's lesson and it's very rude to keep him waiting. He tells me you were learning counting rhymes last week."

"That's right," Roodica sat up and grinned. "And I've just remembered, I made up another rhyme, especially for him."

"Did you?" Her mother was surprised and pleased. "Druid Big Brain will be delighted. You're not usually so keen on your lessons. Do let me hear your rhyme."

Roodica smiled and chanted,

"ONE tWO,
tHE dog did a poo.
THrEE four,
HErE COMES
SOME MORE . . ."

Queen Goodica drew in a deep breath and shuddered. "You will *not* repeat that to Druid Big Brain, Roodica. Do you understand?"

Roodica made a horrible face. "But it's a really good counting rhyme," she muttered. "It took me **ages** to think it up."

She got out of bed, pulled on her linen tunic, then climbed down the ladder into the big hall. Druid Big Brain was standing there with his back to the open fire, chatting to Gideon. He looked up when Roodica approached.

"Good morning, Princess Roodica," he said.

"Hi," Roodica muttered.

Her mother glared at her.

"Hiya?"

The queen grew steely eyed.

Roodica huffed and tried again.

"Good morning, dear Druid Big Brain. And how are you this morning? You're looking awfully well . . . is that better?" she asked her mother.

"Just get on with your lesson," sighed the queen, and picked up her sewing.

"And today's lesson is about the Celtic poets," said the teacher with a great big grin. "We're going to learn all about them and their poetry."

"Just great," muttered Roodica. "Really great."

"It is great," said Gideon. "I like poetry."

"Swot," muttered Roodica. "I hate poetry. It goes on forever. Blah de blah de blah de blah." Then she had one of her brilliant ideas.

"Can I ask you a question, Druid Big Brain?"

"Of course," Druid Big Brain beamed. "I love questions."

"Why are you called Druid Big Brain?"

"Because I am extremely intelligent."

Roodica thought for a moment.

It's not because you've got a big head, then?

No, I . . .

Which matches your big nose.

Well, I . . .

And your big ears. My dad
had a dog once with big ears that were
always wet because they trailed in puddles.
Do your ears trail in puddles? Well no, they
wouldn't, would they, because they're too high
up. Because you're a big person. It's just as well
your feet are big too, isn't it, otherwise you
might topple over, then your ears *would*
trail in the puddles, just like
my dad's dog.

Gideon groaned and put his head in his hands. Druid Big Brain gave Roodica a hard stare, then he smiled.

"My big brain tells me, Princess Roodica, that you are just trying to avoid today's poetry lesson by being sent back to your room for being rude."

"And Druid Big Brain said he would take us swimming in the river if we did well at our lessons today," hissed Gideon.

"Oh, that's different," Roodica perked up, and went and sat at the big table. "Go on then, Druid Big Brain. What was that you were saying about poetry?"

Copius Mucus alias Snot Face

Roodica tried to listen carefully as Druid Big Brain droned on and on about the Celtic poets. Every king seemed to have one. They wrote poems about how clever the king was, poems about how brave the king was, and poems about how good the king was in battle.

"My dad's a king. King Bren. He's

always going off into battle, though I don't think he's very good at it," said Roodica. "Is that why we don't we have a poet?"

Druid Big Brain peered down his long pointed nose at Roodica.

"Ahem. Now that's something I *don't* know," he said.

Roodica thought for a moment.

"Perhaps I could be my dad's poet," she grinned. "I could make up a poem about him. 'Good King Bren ate a big fat . . . duck.' No, that doesn't rhyme. But I did make up a really good counting rhyme . . ."

"*Roodica!*" said the queen, looking up from her sewing.

Roodica huffed and puffed, propped her elbows on the table and rested her chin in her hands. Lesson days were no fun at all. But the queen was keeping a close eye on her so she tried to pay attention. She tried not to watch as Foodica mixed up some pancake batter for lunch. She tried not to watch as Woodica carved out some dainty wooden beads. She nudged Gideon and tried not to giggle as a big hairy spider dropped down from the rafters and hovered on a silken thread, just above Druid Big Brain's bald head. But it was all very difficult.

Eventually Druid Big Brain stopped talking.

"Are there any questions?" he asked.

"Well . . ." Gideon started to say, but Roodica kicked him under the table.

"No questions, Druid Big Brain," she smiled sweetly. "You've made it all very clear. The poets . . . poems . . . poetry . . . thingy."

"Splendid!"

Druid Big Brain announced. "Then I think it's time for us all to go swimming."

"At last," muttered Roodica, jumping up from the table and knocking over Gideon. "COME ON, fleabag, race you to the river!"

"Princesses don't yell," said Queen Goodica, finishing off her sewing.

"Princesses don't run," said Foodica, flipping over her pancakes.

"And Princesses certainly don't race their dogs," said Woodica, stringing her wooden beads.

"This one does," grinned Roodica, as she hitched up her skirt and took off after Fleabag. She ran out through the door

of Maiden Castle and down through the settlement. She dodged ducks and dogs and called to all the settlement children.

"Lessons are finished for the day. I'm going swimming now. **Hooray!**"

"See you at the river later, Roodica," they called back. "We'll come as soon we've finished our chores."

Roodica carried on running and, further down the hill her friend Will,

the blacksmith, gave her a wave, but when she passed the home of her friend, Saddler Sam, he was nowhere to be seen. Someone else was there, though. Someone who was poking about among the gleaming saddles. Someone who was definitely *not* Roodica's friend. That someone was Copius Mucus, the snivelling son of the Roman tax collector.

Roodica frowned. "What are you doing here, Snot Face?" she asked. "These saddles belong to Sam. Get your sticky paws off them or I'll give your nose such a tweak you'll hear it squelch and squeak. Hey, that rhymes," she added in surprise. "I'm a poet and I didn't know it."

Copius snorted. "That's not poetry. You stupid Celts are hopeless at poetry. You need intelligent Romans for that."

"**Rubbish,**" said Roodica. "Druid Big Brain has been telling us all about the Celtic poets."

"Well, that wouldn't take long," sneered Copius. "I've been studying what Suetonius has to say about our great poet, Quintus Horatius Flaccus, for years now."

Roodica gave an enormous pretend yawn. "Who wants to learn what a Suet Pudding has to say about a Squinty Horrible Flatfoot? At least our poets write about fighting and bravery and battles."

"I'm glad to hear you were listening to some of our lesson today, Princess Roodica," smiled Druid Big Brain, appearing at her side with Gideon.

"Yes, and now *we're* all going swimming

and you're not invited, Slimy Chops,"
Roodica said to Copius.

But Copius just sniffed and smiled slyly.
"Going swimming, are you? That's what
you think."

The Disappearing River

Roodica ignored Copius and ran out through the open gate of the stockade and down the hill.

"Hi, Ned," she called to the farmer tending his cattle.

Farmer Ned gave her a wave. She waved back and headed for the bend in the river and her favourite pool. It was bordered by sweet grass and wild flowers and had a large willow tree hanging over it. Roodica loved to climb along the willow's branches and jump into the pool . . . usually on top of Gideon. When Roodica's feet were on the riverbed, the water lapped her chin. But that day, when she finally caught up with Fleabag, she was amazed to see him in the pool with the water just up to his ankles.

"What happened to the river, Fleabag?" she said in amazement. "You didn't drink it all, did you?"

Fleabag rolled his eyes and shook his shaggy head.

"Who stole the river then?" she asked, splashing in after him and looking all round. "Where'd it go?"

Fleabag flicked his eyes from side to side and looked puzzled. He didn't know.

Nor did Gideon when he arrived. "What happened to the river? It was here yesterday when I brought the horses down for a drink."

Even Druid Big Brain shook his head. "There has been plenty of rain," he said.

"The river shouldn't have dried up so quickly. This is a mystery. We must seek out the cause."

"Come on, Fleabag," ordered Roodica. "Get seeking."

Fleabag put his nose to the ground and headed off. The others followed. But they didn't have to go very far. When they rounded the bend they found the river had been dammed by several large oak trees.

"That's very strange," frowned Druid Big Brain. "These trees didn't just fall over. They have been chopped down and dragged here. Look at the flattened grass. Then the trees have been rolled across the river."

Roodica frowned too. "I wonder . . . Fatius Guttus, the Roman tax collector, lives nearby. He recently built a new bath house. I bet he dammed the river to get more water for that."

"I fear you are correct, Princess Roodica, and I fear that must be the end of our swimming lessons. We cannot upset the Romans by removing the trees.

We must accept what has happened. There is nothing we can do."

"Rubbish," muttered Roodica to Gideon, as Druid Big Brain wandered off spouting poetry to himself. "I'm not letting Fatius get away with it. Just who does he think he is? This is *our* river and there is something we can do. I have a brilliant idea, but I need your help."

Gideon looked mutinous.

"I'm not making faces at farmer Ned's bull again to see how mad we can make him. He chased me up a tree the last time."

"Nearly biffed you on the bum, too," giggled Roodica. "I didn't know you

could run that fast. But my idea's not nearly as dangerous as that. We just need to go into the forest and have a chat with Old Mother Silverlocks."

"But she's strange and creepy and really scary," protested Gideon.

"That's true," grinned Roodica. "But at least she can't run as fast as Farmer Ned's bull."

Old Mother Silverlocks. AAARGH!

Roodica, Gideon and Fleabag left the river and slipped into the forest. It sighed and rustled around them as they headed for the cave of Old Mother Silverlocks.

"I don't like this bit of the forest," muttered Gideon, looking all round. "It feels scary."

Then he heard a muffled grunt and a twig SNAP.

"What was that?" he gasped.

"Probably just a wolf or a wild boar or a bear," grinned Roodica. "But don't worry, they won't want to eat you. You're far too skinny."

They trudged on and eventually came to a clearing. In the middle of the clearing was the cave of Old Mother Silverlocks.

"Hello," Roodica called out, peering into the dark cave. "Is there anybody in there?"

There was no reply. The cave was empty.

"She's out," said Gideon. "Let's go."

"Let's wait," said Roodica who started to look around.

"Don't you know it's rude to go poking about in other people's possessions," said Gideon.

"Oh yes," nodded Roodica. "But it's really interesting. I wonder what's in this old pot?"

But before she had a chance to look, a cracked voice rang out:

"Well, my little princess Rude
Who's very very seldom good
Place your hand inside that pot
And you may like it, maybe not.
A slimy frog inside there dwells
For use in my bewitching spells..."

"Quick, put the pot down or she'll turn *you* into a frog. And if that happens, the queen will kill me," cried Gideon. "I knew we shouldn't have come . . ."

"Don't be silly," said Roodica, but she put the pot down anyway as Old Mother Silverlocks hobbled into the cave carrying an armful of firewood.

"Hello, Mother Silverlocks," said Roodica, taking the wood from the old woman and building up the fire. "We've come to see you on a very important matter."

Old Mother Silverlocks nodded.

"Eye of bat and blood of liver
You've seen the disappearing river.
I don't know what's his little game
But I know Fatius is to blame."

Roodica grinned. "I prefer your poetry to Druid Big Brain's. But you're right, and Gideon and I need your help to restore the river."

"So long as I don't end up as an amphibian," muttered Gideon.

"I have a brilliant idea to get Fatius to remove the dam," explained Roodica, "but we need something only you can give us. Something blue."

Old Mother Silverlocks gave a toothless grin.

"Hair of dog and leg of toad
Then what you want from me is woad."

"You're the only one around here who makes the blue dye from the plants," nodded Roodica. "Could I have some?"

"Could I have some, *please*," muttered Gideon.

"Some for him as well," said Roodica. Old Mother Silverlocks regarded her, and a faraway look came into her eye. The left one it was. The other one had gone to sleep.

"Fatius is having important guests. There's bathing, feasting, merry jests ..."

"When? When?" cried Roodica. "It's really important. We must know!"

"The picture's fading, I cannot see
But, by the sun ... about half past three."

"Perfect. We'll set off right away," cried Roodica.

"Hair of dog and leg of toad
Don' t forget the pot of woad."

And Old Mother Silverlocks handed Roodica the old pot she'd been looking at earlier.

"So it didn't contain a slimy frog after all," grinned Roodica when she and

Gideon were safely outside.

"But Old Mother Silverlocks is still really scary," said Gideon. "And she still knew you were in the cave."

"Probably because I left Fleabag parked outside," grinned Roodica. "And everyone knows he goes everywhere with me. But now we've got the woad, the three of us can head for Fatius's villa to try out my brilliant idea."

"Do we have to?" muttered Gideon. "Your brilliant ideas are even worse than Old Mother Silverlocks. They really *are* **scary**."

Helmet Head

Roodica, Gideon and Fleabag followed the river all the way to Fatius's villa and soon found where it flowed in through a lead pipe and into the bath house.

"Just as I thought," muttered Roodica. "Fatius has dammed the river so he can splash about in his stupid bath. Well, we'll soon see about that. Find me a stick, Giddy-up."

"This is no time to be playing fetch with Fleabag," protested Gideon.

"The stick's for emptying out the woad, Birdbrain," said Roodica. "I don't want Fatius or Copius catching me blue-handed."

Gideon broke off a birch twig and Roodica used it to scrape the woad out of the pot and into the river. Fleabag tried to poke his nose into the pot and Gideon had to hold him back.

"How blue are you going to make the water?" Gideon asked.

"As blue as I can," grinned Roodica, and emptied out the entire pot. "Now let's see if my brilliant idea works."

The pair of them watched for a moment as the blue dye spread throughout the river and flowed through the lead pipe. Then with Fleabag's help, they dug a hole and buried the stick and the empty pot under some bushes.

"Come on," said Roodica. "Let's creep nearer the villa and see what happens."

"What happens if we get caught?" asked Gideon.

"I'll say it was all your idea," grinned Roodica.

"WHat!!!"

Roodica and Fleabag led the way as they slipped silently through the trees. Soon the villa came into sight. But something else did too. A big Roman soldier. He was standing guard over several horses and chariots. The horses had been unhitched and were quietly grazing nearby.

"That's it," squeaked Gideon. "Do you see the size of that centurion? I'm out of here."

"No, you're not," said Roodica, hauling him back by the hem of his tunic. "We

just need to get rid of the Helmet Head for a moment and I have a brilliant plan."

"Not another one," groaned Gideon.

Roodica ignored him. "I'll climb up a tree and throw stones at the soldier's helmet. That'll distract him and, when he comes to investigate, you can slip among the horses and quietly scatter them."

"Scatter the horses? Why me?" moaned Gideon.

"Because you're the horse boy, stupid! You're supposed to know about horses!"

Gideon and Fleabag slipped away and Roodica picked up a handful of small pebbles. She hitched up her skirt and climbed up the nearest large oak.

"This should give me good cover," she muttered.

Halfway up she inched out along a stout limb, parted the branches and took careful aim.

the first pebble bounced off the centurion's helmet.

"Don't you mean 'What?'" giggled Roodica, laying very low and still. After a few moments, she eased herself up and threw another pebble.

DING that one bounced off the soldier's breastplate.

The soldier frowned. He looked about then started towards the forest to investigate. As soon as his back was turned Gideon and Fleabag squirmed through the long grass till they reached the horses.

"Go! Go!" Gideon whispered to them, flapping his arms.

But the horses didn't move.

Then Gideon remembered they were Roman horses.

"Vade! Vade!" he tried again.

The horses still ignored him.

"**WUFF**," growled Fleabag.

The horses took one look at the scruffy hound and went galloping off in all directions.

"Great stuff," breathed Roodica.

As soon as she saw that Gideon and

Fleabag were safely back in the forest, she threw the rest of her pebbles at the chariots. **CLACK CLACK CLACK**, they bounced off the sides. The Roman soldier turned then and saw that all the horses had scattered.

"Edepol! Mehercule! O, me miserum!" he exclaimed.

"Yep. You're definitely for it, losing all these horses," giggled Roodica softly.

The soldier took off after the horses and Roodica slid down the tree. Gideon and Fleabag came panting up beside her.

"Well done," she grinned. "I told you my brilliant plan would work. Now let's go and see what's happening in the bath house."

Feeling Blue?

Roodica, Gideon and Fleabag crept towards the bath house. They heard lots of laughing and splashing.

"The Romans are all in the bath already," whispered Roodica. "Come on, follow me."

They sneaked along the edge of the bath house and peeked over the wall.

"Just look at all these people with their

clothes off," whispered Gideon. "They'll catch a terrible cold. All that washing's not good for you. It's not natural. It's not healthy."

"Never mind that, just look at all the food," muttered Roodica. "There's enough there to feed the people in the settlement for a week."

Fleabag's ears pricked up at the mention of food and his great tail waved from side to side, but Roodica motioned him to be still while they waited to see what would happen.

They didn't have to wait for long.

"This really is a splendid party, Fatius," said Magnus Maximus, lolling back in the water with a platter of fruit on his hairy chest. "You've done well."

"Nothing but the best for you, Governor," gushed Fatius.

"And the water's so blue it's almost like being at home in Italy," sighed Dispepsia, the governor's wife.

"Pater had it specially imported from the Tiber in great wooden vats," lied Copius, sneezing onto his bunch of grapes, which fortunately were green anyway.

"That's funny," said Serius Imperius the army chief, examining the water trickling through his gnarled brown fingers. "I used to swim in the Tiber as a boy and I don't remember it being as blue as this."

"Or staining the skin," shrieked his daughter, Hysteria. "Just look at me, I'm blue all over!"

"What? Oh, surely not," cried Fatius. "Maybe you're just a little cold. This dreadful country's always cold, even in the summertime. Or maybe," he squinted up at the sun, "maybe it's a trick of the light."

"A trick anyway," grinned Roodica, as she stole another peek. She saw the guests all leap out of the bath screaming and yelling. They rubbed themselves with their towels and tried to wipe off the woad.

"You stupid idiot, Fatius. We all look like painted barbarians now," yelled Magnus Maximus, scrubbing at his arms.

"And blue is so not my colour," wailed Dispepsia.

"It's not coming off! It's not coming off! I'll be blue for ever," shrieked Hysteria.

"You're such a fathead, Fatius. You haven't heard the last of this!" said Serius Imperius, as he threw on his toga.

"Please don't go," cried Fatius. "I'm sure the blue will wash off. The river must run by some woad plants. I'll remove the dam I made right away."

But it was too late. Fatius's guests, their togas clinging damply to them, had stormed out and were heading for their chariots. But when they got outside, they stopped short. The chariots were there,

but the horses were nowhere to be seen.

"What the ... FATIUS!" they all roared.

Fatius turned pale under the blue stain.

"COPIUS!" he yelled. "Go and find the horses immediately and don't come back without them."

Copius scowled as he set off and Roodica and Gideon grinned as they heard him calling, "Come here, horsey horses, come to Copius. Good horses. Nice horses. Clever horses."

Where are you, you stupid, four-legged mutts?

"**REEESU/t!**" whispered Roodica, as she and Fleabag and Gideon slipped back into the forest and headed for home.

"Now Druid Big Brain can take us swimming again," grinned Roodica, when they were safely back inside the settlement. "And the settlement children will have their pool back too. I told you my brilliant idea would work. I think I may be a genius. I bet my brain is even bigger than Druid Big Brain's."

"Then you'll have no trouble doing your poetry homework for next week," muttered Gideon.

"No trouble at all," said Roodica. "I'm really good at poetry now. I've even made

up a poem for Druid Big Brain. Do you
want to hear it?"

"Do I have to?" muttered Gideon.

Roodica nodded and took a big deep
breath . . .

Damming the river
was crazy and dumb
Now Fatius has a
big blue bum.

"I'm sure Druid Big Brain will like it," she grinned.

ROODICA THE RUDE

by MARGARET RYAN
illustrated by SARAH HORNE

Long ago, when wolves and bears roamed the land,
and before underpants had been invented,
the Romans conquered Britain.

(Romans 1 - Celts 0)

The Romans built fine houses and straight roads,
they encourage the Celts to take baths.

But not everyone liked the Romans. Lots of people
fought back. No one more stubbornly than Queen
Goodica's youngest daughter Roodica the Rude!

SIR QUINTON QUEST

By Kaye Umansky, author of the best selling
Pongwiffy books, illustrated by Judy Brown.

Sir Quinton Quest: world famous explorer, lifelong
member of the Explorers Club, and many-time winner
of the Explorer of the Year Challenge Cup.

Findley Ffoothold: fiendishly good-looking explorer,
successful author and Sir Quinton's arch enemy.
Sir Quinton will do whatever it takes to expose
Ffoothold for the imposter he is – but sometimes his
determination can get in the way of making
the discovery of a lifetime...

by Pete Johnson
illustrated by Mike Gordon

Jamie wishes his annoying little brother,
Harry, would just buzz off and disappear.

But when Jamie becomes the owner
of a magic cape, he soon discovers that he
needs to be careful what he wishes for . . .

You can find out more about other
exciting Catnip books by visiting:
www.catnippublishing.co.uk